Holiday Magic

Suzanne Weyn

PRICE STERN SLOAN
Los Angeles

For Jacqueline Rose Gimmler
with love

Published by Price Stern Sloan, Inc.
11150 Olympic Boulevard
Los Angeles, California 90064
ISBN: 0-8431-3412-7
Printed in the United States of America
10 9 8 7 6 5 4 3 2

Contents

Off to the Mountains

"It is so beautiful up here!" cried Barbie as she steered her red jeep along a curving mountain road. "Look at those snow-covered mountains!"

"I'm so glad you agreed to come with me on this trip," said Kira, sitting beside her.

"No problem," Barbie said. "I've been working hard. A trip is just what I need."

Kira twirled a strand of her long black hair. "Well, I hope it's not the worst winter vacation of your life. My Uncle Ben can be very grouchy."

"It's nice of you to travel all this way to visit him," Barbie said.

"I'm doing it for my aunt Min, really," Kira explained. "She was Uncle Ben's wife. She died almost ten years ago. After that Uncle Ben moved up here to the mountains. He lives alone and doesn't see anyone."

"How sad," said Barbie.

"It is," Kira agreed. "I'm not sure why, but Aunt Min adored Uncle Ben. She wouldn't want him to be alone during the holidays."

"It sounds like she was nice," Barbie said.

"She was," Kira replied. "But Uncle Ben isn't. He's so crabby! I've come up other years, and each time it's the same. It's very hard to talk to him. He gives one-word replies and then stops talking."

"Don't worry," Barbie said cheerfully. "You and I will have him feeling jolly and full of holiday spirit in no time!"

They drove on, up and down snowy mountain roads, until they came to the base of a small mountain. "That's Juniper Hill," said Kira.

Barbie laughed. "Hill? That looks like a pretty big hill to me."

"It's a hill if you look at the huge mountains all around us," Kira said.

A dirt road ran up Juniper Hill. On either side of it were wooden houses shaped like the letter A. Barbie turned her jeep onto the road. "Are these vacation homes?" she asked.

"Some are used by skiers only on the weekends. But I think there are about three families who live here all the time."

Barbie's car bumped along the dirt road. Suddenly the road ended. In front of them was a forest. A mailbox was nailed to a tree, but there was no house in sight.

"Now what?" Barbie asked.

"Now we walk," said Kira. "Uncle Ben lives in a clearing at the top of the hill."

Barbie's blue eyes danced with laughter. "Wow! This is already turning into quite an adventure. Let's go!"

Kira unstrapped her seatbelt. "The town wanted to build a road to the top, but Uncle Ben stopped them. He <u>really</u> wants to be left alone."

"He must care about the forest," said Barbie as she pulled a fuzzy pink cap over her long blond hair.

"No," Kira said. "He cares about being left alone."

Barbie took her overnight bag from the backseat and got out of the car. "Lead the way," she told Kira.

With their bags slung over their shoulders, they walked into the forest. Full green pines and bare birch trees stood close together. Only a little late-afternoon sunlight made it through the thick pine branches. "This reminds me of a magical forest I read about when I was small," said Barbie. "It's so lovely."

They walked on, climbing over fallen trees and up small rocky slopes. "Look at all these tracks in the snow," Barbie said. The tracks of birds, squirrels and other animals they couldn't name crisscrossed one another.

"Check these out," said Kira, pointing to the ground. "These look like rabbit tracks. But they're really big."

Barbie looked at the tracks. "They might be tracks of a snowshoe hare. I've seen them. They get pretty large."

"Well, it looks like this snowshoe hare was being followed by something even larger." Running alongside the line of hare tracks was another set of tracks.

Barbie studied the second tracks. "Some animal with sharp claws must have been tracking the hare." She glanced around. "See over there, behind that fallen tree? The clawed-prints are alone for a while. Then they start following the hare. It must have picked up the hare's scent right here."

"Could it have been a bear?" Kira asked.

"Bears sleep in winter," Barbie reminded her. "Maybe a wolf or a fox."

Kira got to her feet. "A wolf?" she said, gulping. "Let's keep moving."

Finally they came to a clearing. "That's his house," said Kira, pointing.

"Oh, my gosh!" cried Barbie. Before them, at the very top of the hill, was a large square house. An open porch wrapped around it. Pink glints of the newly setting sun bounced off its many windows.

A stunning, snow-covered landscape surrounded them. "This is breathtaking," Barbie said.

At that moment, a short, stocky figure appeared on the porch.

Kira waved. "Uncle Ben!" she shouted.

For a second the man stared at them. Then he turned and vanished into the house.

2

Uncle Ben

Kira banged on the front door. "Uncle Ben!" she shouted. Barbie and Kira had been standing at the door for more than five minutes.

"Maybe he didn't know it was you," said Barbie.

"He knew," Kira insisted. "I wrote him that we were coming." Kira banged two more times. "He's just hoping I'll go away."

"Then perhaps we should," Barbie said.

"I've come all this way. I'm going to spread a little holiday cheer whether he likes it or not," said Kira.

Kira and Barbie looked at each other for a moment—then they both burst out laughing. The idea of forcing someone to be full of holiday spirit suddenly seemed very silly. "Oh, maybe you're right," said Kira.

"We can get a hotel room," Barbie said as they began walking away from the house.

Just then, the door swung open. A short, balding man with a wrinkled face stood in the doorway. "Hello, Kira," he said.

"Hello, Uncle Ben," said Kira, turning toward him. "This is my friend Barbie."

Uncle Ben nodded politely. An awkward silence followed. "It's kind of cold out here," Kira hinted.

"Oh, yes...please come in," he said.

Uncle Ben's home was simple but lovely. There were no curtains on the windows. The pink and gold sunset now colored everything in the room. Barbie had the feeling of being indoors and outside at the same time.

Uncle Ben's dark eyes darted from Kira to Barbie. He seemed to be studying them.

"So, how have you been?" Kira asked with forced cheerfulness.

"Been fine," Uncle Ben replied.

"We saw some strange tracks on the way up," Kira said. "You don't have wolves around here, do you?"

Uncle Ben nodded. "One wolf. He is very mean. Very dangerous."

"Oh," said Kira. "Luckily we didn't meet up with him."

There was another long, awkward pause.

Boy, thought Barbie. Now I see why Kira wanted company. It's not easy to talk with Uncle Ben.

"Your home is beautiful," she said, filling in the silence. "Could I see the rest?"

"Come," said Uncle Ben.

Barbie and Kira followed Uncle Ben out of the room. "Good move," Kira whispered to Barbie. "He's very proud of this place."

Uncle Ben showed Barbie and Kira his large home. Every room was simple and tasteful. "What's in that room?" Barbie asked as they passed a closed door on the second floor.

"My workshop," Uncle Ben replied, passing the door without opening it.

"What kind of work?" Barbie asked.

"I fix things," Uncle Ben answered quickly.

He took them to the basement. "Wait till you see this," Kira said in Barbie's ear. "This is his storage room."

Barbie's eyes widened in amazement. Uncle Ben had stocked his basement with food and supplies. A large freezer stood in the corner. The walls were lined with shelves, and the shelves were crammed with canned goods.

"Gee," said Barbie. "I guess you don't have to go shopping much."

Uncle Ben shook his head. "I go twice a year."

That night Kira offered to cook. Despite all the food in the supply room, there was very little in the kitchen. Kira went to the basement and returned with frozen chicken wings and vegetables. She made a wonderful dinner.

After dinner, Uncle Ben bid them good night.

"You may use the bedroom at the top of the stairs," he said as he left.

Barbie and Kira headed for the bedroom. "Tomorrow we'll give him his presents and then go," said Kira as she changed into her nightshirt.

"I'm in no hurry," Barbie said, yawning. The drive had tired her. She curled up under the covers and quickly fell asleep. Just before dawn, she opened her eyes. Outside the window, a heavy snow was falling. Rubbing her eyes, Barbie went to the window and watched the magical sight.

It's beautiful, Barbie thought. But I hope it stops before morning. I wouldn't want to drive in that snow.

She turned to go back to bed, but something made her stop. It was a sound. The sound of a wolf howling.

3

A Winter Wonderland

"I don't believe this," said Kira, looking out the bedroom window. By morning, the snow flurries had turned into a full blizzard. At least ten inches of snow had fallen. And it was still falling! The lovely view of the mountains was gone. All Barbie and Kira could see was the thick, white, falling snow.

"Maybe it will stop soon," Barbie said as she dressed.

"I sure hope so," said Kira. "No offense to Uncle Ben, but hanging around with him is not my idea of fun! I want to leave."

They finished dressing and went to the kitchen. Kira searched for some breakfast food. "One box of cereal and a box of powdered milk," she said, wrinkling her nose. "We could go see what he's got stashed in the basement."

"The cereal is OK," Barbie said. "I guess Uncle Ben is still sleeping."

But at that moment, the old man walked into the room. His heavy, hooded parka was blanketed with snow.

"Hi," said Barbie. "How is it outside?"

"Still snowing hard," he said.

"I'd offer to make you a cup of tea or something, but I don't see any," Kira hinted, wanting a cup for herself as well.

"I don't drink tea," Uncle Ben said, taking off his parka. "And I've already eaten. It is not healthy to sleep late."

"Late!" Kira cried. "It's seven-thirty."

"I get up when the day begins," replied Uncle Ben. "Now, you will excuse me. I have work to do." With that, he left the room.

"What a fun guy," Kira joked when he was gone. "Let's get out of here. OK?"

"Sure, if you want to," Barbie said as she poured some flakes into a bowl. "But why don't we stay another day? Your uncle just needs time to get used to us. He hasn't seen you all year, and he doesn't know me. Maybe he's a little shy."

"I don't think so," said Kira. "He clearly does not want us here.. We don't like being here. So why stay?"

"It's up to you," Barbie said. "You know him better than I do."

After finishing their cereal, they packed up and put on their hats, coats, gloves and boots. "I want to say good-bye to Uncle Ben, but I don't even know where he went," Kira said, looking around.

"We could try his workroom," Barbie suggested. "What does he fix?"

Kira shrugged. "As far as I know, he's a retired landscaper. Maybe he just fixes things that break." They walked to his workroom. Kira rapped on the closed door. "Uncle Ben," she called.

There was no reply.

Barbie tilted her head and listened. "I don't hear anything. I guess he's not in there."

"Hmmm, I wonder where he went," said Kira. "Well, I'm not waiting around for him. I'll leave him a note."

Kira wrote a thank-you note. She left it with Uncle Ben's presents on the kitchen table.

"How pretty!" cried Kira when they stepped outside into the falling snow.

"Look at this!" cried Barbie. She had stepped knee-deep into a snowdrift. "It's not going to be easy to get to the car."

"Do you want to spend Christmas away from Skipper and Ken?" Kira asked.

"Not really," said Barbie.

"Let's go then," said Kira.

They slogged through the thick, wet snow. Despite the weather, they were in good moods.

"There's something about snow that always makes me happy," Barbie said as they stepped out of the clearing and into the trees.

"Until you have to shovel it," said Kira. "But I know what you mean."

It was easier to walk among the trees since the snow wasn't as deep. The pines formed a sort of roof over their heads and kept out some of the falling snow. They walked in silence for a while. Kira finally spoke. "Barbie? I have the weird feeling that I'm being watched."

Barbie looked at her sharply. "I was just thinking the exact same thing."

They stopped and looked around. Kira clutched Barbie's jacket with her gloved hand. "I don't like this, Barbie."

Suddenly a loud snap broke the quiet. A branch had grown too heavy with snow and split off from the tree.

Barbie and Kira whirled around to look at it. Then the branch broke completely. It crashed to the ground. As it did, a large, gray animal scrambled away from the tree.

"Did you see that?" cried Kira. "It was the wolf! The wolf was watching us!"

"I did see it," said Barbie. "I'm surprised he came so close."

They hurried on. When they came to the place where the road ended, Barbie looked for her jeep. For a moment, she thought it had disappeared. Then she spotted it. "It looks like a car for a snowman," she said. It was completely covered by snow.

Kira went to the car and began brushing off the thick snow. "We'll have this cleared in a jiff!"

"Don't bother," said Barbie. "We're not going anywhere."

Kira followed Barbie's gaze. "So I see," she said. The road was completely snowed under!

4

The Beast-Man

Barbie gazed out of Uncle Ben's living room window. After a long hike, she and Kira had finally made their way back.

Uncle Ben had not looked happy when they knocked on his door. Kira was just as unhappy. "Don't they plow the roads around here?" she asked in a grouchy voice.

"I do not know," said Uncle Ben. Then he returned to his workroom.

As Barbie watched the falling snow, Kira plunked down on the couch. She took a beaded jacket from her canvas tote. "At least now I have the time to finish sewing the beads on this," she said. She took out her sewing kit and threaded the needle. "I finished the rest of the dress. I just hope I get home in time to wear it for the holidays."

"You'll be home in time," said Barbie. Kira's new dress still stood on a form in Barbie's sewing room. Kira had borrowed Barbie's sewing machine. "It came out beautifully," Barbie added.

"Thanks," said Kira.

Kira began sewing the beads onto her jacket. Barbie wandered down the hall. The day before, she hadn't looked closely at the paintings on the wall. Now she had the time. Most of them were pictures of nature— mountains, birds, woodland animals. They seemed to have been done by the same artist. Yet they weren't signed. "Who did the artwork?" Barbie called to Kira.

"Gee, I don't know," Kira replied.

Barbie kept going down the hall. She came to a room lined with bookshelves from ceiling to floor. The day before, Uncle Ben had whisked them past this room. Now Barbie went in and gazed at the books.

Taking a book called *The Winter Woods* from the shelf, Barbie went back to the living room. She settled down next to Kira on the couch.

"I wonder what your uncle does in his workroom," Barbie said. "I think he's pretty interesting. His house is so lovely. He's so quiet and mysterious."

"He's quiet because he can't be bothered talking to people," said Kira.

"Was he always like that?" Barbie asked.

"I was so young that it's hard to remember," Kira said, putting down her sewing. "He was always quiet, but before Aunt Min died he used to smile easily."

"He must miss her a lot," said Barbie.

Kira went back to sewing, and Barbie opened the large book on her lap. It was filled with glossy color photos. One chapter talked about winter wildlife. Another named all the winter birds in the area—the hairy woodpecker, the chickadee, the cedar waxwing.

The book inspired Barbie. After a while, she wanted to go back out and see the winter woods for herself. "Want to do a little hiking?" she asked Kira.

Kira set aside her sewing. "Why not?"

"I saw some snowshoes in the closet by the front door," said Barbie. "I don't think Uncle Ben will mind if we borrow them."

After dressing warmly, they strapped on the snowshoes and went back outside. The snow was still falling hard. Back in the forest, Barbie looked at it with a fresh eye. She saw small tracks in the snow. She listened and heard the calls of birds.

"Barbie, look," said Kira. "Do you think those are wolf tracks?"

Barbie crouched and looked at the tracks. "They're the same tracks we saw near the hare tracks the other day."

"I don't like the sound of that," Kira said.

She checked around for the wolf. "Let's keep moving."

They reached the edge of the forest. Barbie's car was buried more deeply in snow than before. "I should start the car just to warm it up a little," said Barbie.

"Good idea," agreed Kira.

As Barbie went to her car, she noticed the tops of three colorful woolen caps peeking up from behind the trunk. Two boys and a smaller girl were hiding there.

"Hi," Barbie greeted them.

With terror-filled eyes, they jumped up and ran away—screaming at the top of their voices.

5

Tough Times

As they ran, the little girl slipped and fell in the snow. Barbie hurried to help her up.

"Leave her alone!" shouted the taller of the two boys. They had stopped and stood about two yards away. All three children had red hair and freckles. It was easy to see that they were brothers and sister.

"Don't hurt me," begged the girl, who looked about four. Barbie let go of the girl's arm, and she ran quickly to the boys.

"We wouldn't hurt you," said Kira, coming up behind Barbie. "Why are you scared of us?"

"You're friends of the beast-man!" the girl shouted.

"The what?" Kira laughed.

"The beast-man who lives on the hill," said the younger boy, who looked about five.

"He's not a beast," said Barbie.

"Oh, yes, he is," the girl insisted. "Our mom said to stay away from him. At night he turns into a wolf and eats people."

"Your mom told you that?" Barbie questioned.

"Not the wolf part," said the older boy, who was about seven. "But she said we should stay away from him."

"He does turn into a wolf," the girl said. "I hear him howling at night."

"Listen," Barbie said, changing the subject. "Do you know when they're planning to plow this road?"

The kids shook their heads. "I hope it's soon," said the oldest boy. "Mom was going to go grocery shopping today."

"Maybe their mom knows when the snowplows are coming," Kira said to Barbie.

"Could we talk to her?" Barbie asked the kids.

The kids whispered to one another. "Are you beast-girls?" the five-year-old asked.

"We're not. We promise," Barbie answered, trying not to laugh.

"OK, then," said the boy. Kira and Barbie followed the kids down to the nearest house. They stepped up onto a porch that was piled high with firewood. "Hey, Mom!" the oldest boy called at the door. "Some people to see ya!"

A woman with the same red hair and freckles came to the door. "Hi," said Barbie. "I'm Barbie and this is Kira. We're staying just up the hill. We were wondering if you knew when the plows were coming."

The woman invited them in. "Pleased to meet you. I'm Mary Dill. I wish I knew the answer to your question. The phone lines are down right now. But the plows usually start over by the ski resort and work their way to us. It might take days."

"Days!" Kira groaned.

"I'm afraid so," said Mrs. Dill. "I'm out of everything. If I can't get food, I'm going to be in trouble." She stole a sidelong glance at her kids. They were busy pulling off their jackets. "I haven't gotten any Christmas shopping done yet, either. It's going to be pretty disappointing if I don't get out by Christmas. Besides that, my husband is away on a sales trip. Now he can't get back."

"But Christmas is four days away," said Barbie. "Do you think we'll be stuck here that long?"

"The last time we had a blizzard like this, we were snowed-in for five days."

"How are the other people on the hill doing?" Kira asked.

"I don't know," said Mrs. Dill.

"Why don't we take a walk down and talk to some of them?" Barbie said to Kira.

"OK," Kira agreed. "By the way," she said to Mrs. Dill, "why do the kids think my uncle turns into a wolf?"

"They saw a big gray wolf right near his house late one afternoon," she explained. "It scared them good. Scared me, too, when they told me. They're not allowed to go up there and bother your uncle, anyway."

Barbie and Kira said good-bye to Mary Dill. They trudged down the hill to see Mrs. Fein. The small woman came to the door leaning on a cane. "How nice to have guests," she said, greeting them.

"My children and grandchildren were supposed to come yesterday for the end of Hanukkah. But they called and said the airport here is closed. They don't know when it will open again."

"What a shame," said Barbie.

Across the way from Mrs. Fein was a black family with two small girls. Mr. Blaine was clearing his front walk when Barbie and Kira arrived. "I've been trying to clear this walkway since this morning," he said, laughing. "But it keeps snowing faster than I can shovel."

John Blaine was most worried about his fuel tanks. "We're low on oil. If I run out, I can't get a fuel truck up here. It'll be a cold holiday if that happens."

"Is there anything you can do?" Kira asked.

"Turn the heat down, keep the fireplace burning and hope for the best," he said.

On the way back, Barbie and Kira walked in silence. "Uncle Ben has plenty of supplies stored up there," said Kira after a while.

"That's what I was thinking," said Barbie. "Would he be willing to share?"

"I doubt it," Kira replied. "He doesn't want anything to do with his neighbors."

"I'm going to ask him," said Barbie.

"Good luck," Kira said. "You'll need it."

6

The Secret in the Workroom

It was late afternoon when Barbie and Kira got back to the house. "My fingers are freezing," Kira complained. "Do you think Uncle Ben would care if we lit a fire?"

"I'll go ask," said Barbie. "Maybe he's still in his workroom."

Barbie went to the room. The door had swung open a crack. Through the crack she saw an alarming sight.

Uncle Ben lay slumped at a table!

"Oh, dear!" cried Barbie, rushing in. Her heart pounded. What was the matter?

Then she heard his snores. She realized he was simply sleeping. What a relief, she thought, sighing.

Barbie looked around. Uncle Ben had fallen asleep at a long worktable. But he wasn't fixing things. He was carving. Tiny wooden birds were perched on the table. Some were brightly painted and sat atop charming handmade birdhouses.

Gently, Barbie picked up a small carved bird. "A chickadee," she said, recalling the bird from Uncle Ben's book. "And a cedar waxwing and a hairy woodpecker," she added, looking at the other carved birds on the table.

At the sleeping man's side was a sketch pad. Rough drawings of the birds were done with charcoal. Uncle Ben had sketched the birds from the forest. Then he brought his drawings back and turned them into carvings. It struck Barbie that the paintings in the hall also must have been done by Uncle Ben.

Barbie shifted her gaze to the walls. They were lined with photos. The early ones were in black and white. Later ones were in color. They all had one thing in common. They were all of Uncle Ben and a pretty dark-haired woman.

"This must be Aunt Min," Barbie murmured.

Suddenly, the old man sputtered in his sleep. Barbie jumped back. She didn't want him to awaken and find her in the room.

Heading quickly for the door, Barbie saw something on the floor. It was a charcoal sketch—of a wolf's head.

She remembered the little Dill girl. The girl had been so sure Uncle Ben turned into a wolf.

"Don't be silly," Barbie scolded herself. She put the drawing on a side table and left the room.

Kira and Barbie made a fire without waiting for Uncle Ben. Barbie told Kira about the workroom. "I've always wondered about that room too," Kira said. "I'd never have guessed he was an artist."

They went down to the supply room to find food for supper. Barbie noticed a stack of metal drums. "He's got barrels of fuel oil here," she said. "This would sure help the Blaines."

Kira's arms were full with frozen vegetables, french fries and hamburger patties. "The Dills could use some of this food right now, too."

They went back upstairs and started making dinner. Soon Uncle Ben came into the kitchen. Barbie was dying to ask him about his artwork. But she wasn't supposed to know about it.

Dinner was mostly silent. In bursts of talk, both Kira and Barbie tried to be friendly. But Uncle Ben simply gave one-word replies. Barbie tried to work up the nerve to talk to him about his neighbors.

Finally, at the end of the meal, she spoke up. She told him all about their trip down the hill. He listened silently, showing no feeling. "You can't solve all their problems," Barbie said. "But if you could spare some food for the Dills and some fuel for the Blaines, it might help."

"The winters here can be harsh," he said when she was done.

"I knew you would understand!" she cried.

"No. It is you who does not understand," he said sharply. "These people chose to live here. They should know the ways of the mountains. It is not my fault that they are not prepared. If I give my supplies, then I will be caught short."

"But..." Barbie began. It was no use. Uncle Ben was already on his feet.

"Good night," he said. "Thank you for fixing the meal."

Barbie frowned, watching him leave. "Who would think such an unpleasant man could do such lovely artwork?"

That night, the snow stopped. "I bet we'll be out of here tomorrow," Kira said as she looked out the bedroom window. "The road will be plowed by then."

With a sleepy yawn, Barbie nodded. "I hope you're right." She fell asleep and dreamed of wolves. In the middle of the night she opened her eyes. A sound had awakened her.

At first she thought she must still be dreaming. Then she sat up. She <u>had</u> heard it. It was the howl of a wolf.

Going to the window, she looked out. The snow had started again. From behind the clouds, a streak of silver moonlight made the flakes shine.

Suddenly, a large, gray animal darted across the snowy field of whiteness. She saw it clearly. It was a wolf.

7

A Change of Heart

In the morning, Barbie woke early. The snow was still falling. She wiped a circle in the steamy window and saw Uncle Ben trudging toward the woods.

Kira was still asleep. Quietly, Barbie let herself out of the room and went to the kitchen.

Set out on the table was a large box. It was crammed with food—powdered milk, flour, cocoa, frozen meats and vegetables, bottles of juice. A piece of paper lay on top of the food. The words "Deliver these" were written on it. "Well, what do you know," Barbie said to herself.

She ran and woke Kira. "Come on. We have an errand to run," she said.

"What do you mean?" Kira asked, sleepily.

Barbie dragged her out of bed. "Come see."

In the kitchen, Kira danced around the table. "You did it, Barbie. There's only one problem. How do we lift it?"

"I have an idea," Barbie said. Kira and Barbie dressed. Together, they dragged the box to the front door. "I'll be right back," said Barbie. She ran to the side of the house. In a moment she returned, dragging a sled. "Yesterday I noticed this leaning against the house.

They put the box on the sled and headed down the hill through the forest. Soon they came to the end of the woods where Barbie's snow-covered car stood. "What's that by my car?" Barbie wondered aloud. By her right tire was another sled. On the sled was one of Uncle Ben's metal barrels of fuel oil. Barbie ran to it. "He must have brought it down for us early in the morning."

Kira shook her head with astonishment. "It must be you, Barbie. I've never seen him do anything like this."

They dragged the sled of food down to the Dills' house. It took the two of them to get it up onto the porch.

"Bless you!" cried Mary Dill when she saw what they'd brought. "This morning I pulled out my last bag of flour. For the life of me, I didn't know what I was going to do. Thank you so very much."

"You're welcome, but the food is really from Ben up the hill," said Barbie.

"The beast-man?" cried the girl they'd seen the day before.

"Caitlin, don't be rude," Mary scolded her.

"I'm not. I saw him from my window last night. He ran right by the house," the girl insisted.

Mary laughed. "Kids," she said, shaking her head. "Tell Ben we are so grateful."

Their next stop was to bring the barrel of oil to the Blaines. When they knocked on the door, Mrs. Blaine answered, wrapped in a heavy blanket. Looking past her shoulder, Barbie saw two little girls, also wrapped in blankets, sitting near the fireplace.

"This is too good to be true," said Julia Blaine when Kira and Barbie told her what they'd brought.

"We were down to our last drop of oil," John Blaine said, coming out to get the barrel. "This will get me through another day. Maybe two, if we're careful. Thank you."

"I wish we had something for Mrs. Fein," Kira said as they walked away from the Blaine home. "She seems so lonely."

Barbie's eyes brightened. "We do have something for her. Company!"

"You're right," said Kira. "Let's go."

After their visit with Mrs. Fein, they trudged back up the hill. The snow had stopped for the moment. When they passed the Dill home, Mary called out to them.

She ran down to the road. "We baked these

cookies for Ben and for you," she said, handing them a plate of colorful cookies. "And the children drew these cards." She gave them a large envelope filled with the handmade cards.

"These will make Ben happy," said Barbie.

Barbie was quiet as she dragged the empty sled back through the forest.

"What are you thinking?" Kira asked.

"I was thinking that Uncle Ben did a really nice thing today. Perhaps we could spread some holiday cheer to him." She began breaking off some greens from the branches. "We have everything we need here."

"I'm following you," said Kira. She knelt and picked up a snow-covered pinecone. She tossed it onto the sled. "Let's go all out. He'll be in his workroom, I bet. It'll be a surprise. He'll probably hate it and throw us out into the blizzard, but..."

"But, hey!" Barbie said laughing. "At least we'll have tried."

8

Surprises!

Barbie and Kira were swept up in excitement and full of holiday ideas. By the time they pulled the sled out of the woods, it was piled high with pine branches and pinecones. They had even found a holly bush with shiny red berries.

Back at the quiet house, they twisted the branches into a wreath. They used paperclips to tie the branches and attach the pinecones. Barbie took a red scarf from her suitcase and tied it in a bow. "Perfect," she said as she attached the bow to the wreath and hung it over the fireplace. They arranged the holly on the mantel.

Down in the supply room, they found popcorn kernels and a bag of whole frozen cranberries. They popped the corn. Then, using Kira's sewing kit, they strung the popcorn and cranberries. "We have the garlands but no tree," said Barbie when they were done.

So back they went into the forest with the empty sled and an ax they'd found among Uncle Ben's supplies. In an hour, they returned, dragging a fat, blue-green fir tree. It took them another hour to rig up a tree stand. They used an upside-down crate with a hole cut in it, set over a basin of water. With some help from the corner walls, the tree finally stood. Before long, they had it circled with the garlands.

After lighting a fire, they stood back and admired their work.

Just then, Uncle Ben came out of his workroom. He stared at the tree and the wreath. "Do you like it?" Kira asked.

He didn't answer, as though he hadn't heard her. He kept staring at the tree.

"The Dills sent you these," said Barbie, handing him the plate of cookies. "And they made cards, too."

Uncle Ben handed back the cookies and took the cards. Barbie watched as he sorted through them. There was a picture of Santa and one of a Christmas tree. But then Uncle Ben came to the oddest of the cards. It was a crayon picture of a wolf. In large, scraggly letters were printed the words "Thank yu beest man from Caitlin."

Uncle Ben's eyes narrowed in confusion.

"She thinks you turn into a wolf at night," Barbie told him gently.

Uncle Ben looked sharply at Barbie. "She does?"

"She's just a little girl," said Barbie. "You know how kids are."

Barbie wasn't sure, but it seemed that the old man's eyes were wet with tears. "Are you OK?" she asked.

"Mmmm," he grunted. Then he turned and left the room.

"I guess our holiday cheer didn't go over too big," said Kira.

Barbie sighed. "I suppose not." With glum faces, they plopped down on the couch. "At least <u>we</u> can enjoy it. It looks like we may be spending Christmas here."

"I'm sorry I got you into this, Barbie," Kira said. "You won't see Skipper or Ken for the holiday. Oh, and I just remembered! That amazing dress you bought. You won't get to wear it!"

"Oh, well, there's always next year," said Barbie. "We're no worse off than the rest of the people on the hill. The Dills won't see their father. Mrs. Fein can't visit with her family. And the Blaines are stuck there by themselves."

As they spoke, Uncle Ben came back into the room holding a box. "The tree needs ornaments," he said. "I have these from many years ago."

Barbie and Kira got up and looked into the box. "How pretty," said Barbie, looking at the brightly colored glass balls.

Kira gasped. "Aunt Min's collection. I remember these balls. She loved them."

"Yes, each year I gave her a new one," said Uncle Ben. He set the box on a chair and began hanging them on the tree. He spoke without looking at them. "Having you girls here reminds me of when Min was alive. It is almost like old times."

I knew I was right about him, thought Barbie. He's not as tough as he pretends.

Just then she had a great idea!

"I was thinking," she said to Uncle Ben. "Everyone on the hill is having a tough time. A party would cheer us all up. We could have it here."

Uncle Ben whirled around. "No! No! I know nothing of how to give a party."

"We'd do all the work," said Kira.

Uncle Ben folded his arms stubbornly. "You girls may make a party. But do not expect me to attend. Neighbors bring trouble. I do not want to know them."

"But you might like..." Barbie began. But Uncle Ben wasn't listening. He walked past her out of the room.

"Nice try," Kira said. "For a minute there, he almost seemed human."

"He's very human," Barbie said thoughtfully. "I say we go ahead and have the party."

9

An Unexpected Guest

The next day was Christmas Eve. The snow had finally stopped falling. Barbie and Kira got up early and went down the hill. They invited everyone on the hill to the party.

"Too bad Mrs. Fein won't be able to get up the hill," Barbie said as they returned home.

"Maybe we'll think of something. In the meantime, we'd better get to work. We have a lot to do," Kira said.

The food they had brought up from the supply room was set out on the kitchen table. They had a canned ham, sweet potatoes and the fixings for punch. They planned to make cookies and lots of hot snacks. They quickly got to work. Uncle Ben came out of his workroom at lunchtime. He made a sandwich for himself. "This is going to be fun," Barbie said to him.

"I won't be there," he replied as he left.

At four-thirty, Barbie was sprinkled with flour from her last batch of cookies. Suddenly, she heard a buzzing sound in the distance. She stood still and listened.

"It sounds like a power saw," said Kira.

"But the sound is getting louder," Barbie noticed. "It's as if it's getting closer." Dusting the flour off her hands, Barbie looked out the window. The sound was now quite loud. Barbie stared out across the snowy field. A man riding a snowmobile came out of the forest. She watched as he headed for the house. When he was almost there, her heart leapt.

"Ken!" she cried. She grabbed her jacket and squirmed into it as she ran out into the snow.

"What are you doing here?" she cried happily when she met his snowmobile.

Ken shut off the engine. "Are you OK? I was worried."

Barbie threw her arms around him. "You're

so sweet! I would have called, but all the phone lines are down. Where did you get the snowmobile?"

"I rented it in town. It's a mess down there. Cars are stuck all over the place. They're working like mad just to keep the roads clear."

"Which means the plows won't get here soon," said Barbie.

"I wouldn't count on it," said Ken.

Barbie hopped on behind Ken. Together they rode the rest of the way to the house.

Barbie saw that a large duffle bag was strapped on behind her. "You sure brought enough stuff," she teased.

"I was about to leave with just a sweater. Then I stopped by your house to check on your sister," said Ken as he stopped the snowmobile.

"Is Skipper OK?" Barbie asked.

"She's fine. But she insisted that you needed a ton of stuff."

"Good old Skipper," Barbie said, laughing.

Ken lugged the heavy bag into the house. "Hey, Ken!" Kira greeted him in the living room. "I can't believe you came all this way."

"I heard on the news that you were snowed in," he explained. "I got worried when you didn't call."

"That's so nice of you," said Kira. She glanced at Ken's duffle bag. "What did you bring? Your entire wardrobe?"

"This is stuff Skipper sent," said Barbie. She unzipped the bag. The first item she pulled out was a long deep-green velvet dress with high puffed sleeves and red, white and green sequins down the front. It was Barbie's new holiday dress! "She even remembered the matching bag and bow!" Barbie said excitedly.

"She said you'd be bummed out if you didn't get to wear it," Ken said.

"I <u>was</u> sort of sad about not getting to wear it," Barbie admitted.

Next Barbie pulled out a long hot-pink gown. "Skipper put that in for you, Kira," said Ken.

Kira picked up the dress. "It's my holiday dress. And now I have the jacket finished!"

"I'm glad she thought to do that," said Barbie. "After all your work, it would have been a shame not to get to wear it."

"Excuse me," said Ken, "But where are you planning to wear these dresses?"

"To our party, of course," Kira said.

"Party?" cried Ken.

"Of course. It's Christmas Eve," Barbie said, smiling. "Could you please get Mrs. Fein? She's an old lady, and has no way to get here."

"You guys are amazing," said Ken. "I came up expecting you to be starving or freezing. And instead you're having a party."

"Well, speaking of parties, it's after five," said Barbie. "We'd better get dressed."

10

The Wolf Appears

At a quarter to six, Barbie and Kira were dressed and ready for their guests. They had brought the kitchen table into the living room and laid out all the food. Aunt Min's Christmas balls sparkled on the tree.

"I'll be right back," Barbie said. She went to Uncle Ben's workroom and knocked on the door. "Won't you change your mind?" she called in to him.

"No. Please go away," he shouted.

Disappointed, Barbie turned and went back to the living room. Ken had just returned with Mrs. Fein. "A ride up on a snowmobile!" the old woman said, laughing. "That's what I call an adventure!"

The next to arrive were the Dills. Once they peeled off their snow gear, they were dressed in their holiday finest. "Caitlin, don't stand there in the doorway," Mary Dill scolded gently.

"But Mom, I'm scared of the beast-man," Caitlin said, her voice trembling.

"Don't be silly," said Mary, guiding her daughter into the room.

Shortly after the Dills, the Blaines arrived. Little Tiffany and Amy Blaine wore matching red velvet dresses.

"Come in," Barbie greeted them. "We're so happy you could come."

"Where's your uncle?" John Blaine asked Kira. "I want to thank him for the fuel."

"I'm afraid he isn't feeling up to a party tonight," Kira said.

"Oh, that's a shame," said John.

The party got off to a great start. The kids played and laughed. The adults all chatted merrily.

Then, in the middle of the happy chatting

came a piercing scream. "There he is!" cried Caitlin, pointing out the window. "The beast-man."

The guests rushed to the window. A fat full moon hung low in the sky. In its light stood a large wolf.

"My gosh," murmured Mary. "Why is that wolf so close to the house?"

In the next minute they saw Uncle Ben, walking across the gleaming white snow. He was headed straight for the wolf.

"Oh, my! What is he doing?" cried Julia Blaine. "That wolf could attack him!"

But instead, Uncle Ben went very close to the wolf and tossed a slab of red meat to him. While the wolf gobbled the meat, Uncle Ben walked calmly back to the house.

"You see," Barbie said to Caitlin. "The wolf is his friend. But Ben isn't a wolf."

Caitlin nodded. "I never knew a man who had a wolf for a friend," she said.

"Neither have I," Barbie agreed softly.

The guests went back to their party. "Come and get some of this food," Kira told them. As they ate, Barbie heard a door open and shut. She saw Uncle Ben slip past and down the hall.

After they ate, Barbie suggested they sing carols. Mrs. Fein pulled a harmonica from her small velvet purse. "I can play a few holiday tunes on this," she said. Everyone gathered near the fire and sang. Barbie sat beside Ken and held his hand.

While they were singing "Deck the Halls" the voices began to trail off. First the children stopped singing. Then the adults. Barbie turned to see what they were looking at.

Uncle Ben had come into the room. In his arms was a cardboard box.

"Are we being too loud?" Kira asked.

"No," he said. "I liked the singing. I haven't heard these songs in a long time."

"Then why don't you join us?" said John Blaine, getting up from his seat.

"Perhaps, but I..." Uncle Ben seemed very shy. "I have brought some things for the children. Little things."

Excitedly, the kids gathered around him. To each of them, he gave one of his carved birdhouses with the birds on top.

"Yours is a little different," Uncle Ben said to Caitlin. He handed her the present. It was a carved box with a wooden figure of a wolf on top. "I made it just for you."

"Thank you," Caitlin said.

"You see, I feed my wolf friend because in winter, food is not easy to find," he explained. "I don't want him to bother other people. He might scare them and get himself shot."

"You mean the wolf is really nice?" Caitlin asked, staring at the box.

"He's not as mean as he seems," Uncle Ben replied.

Mrs. Fein blew a note on her harmonica. Everyone began singing "We Wish You a Merry Christmas" in loud, happy voices. Uncle Ben joined in quietly but happily, his eyes shining.

When the song ended, Uncle Ben went to the table. He poured himself a cup of soda. "I would like to toast our two hostesses. They have warmed an old man's heart and made a bright holiday."

"Thanks," said Kira. "But this party was Barbie's idea. She deserves the credit."

"To Barbie, then," said Uncle Ben, raising his glass.

The guests all toasted. "To Barbie!"

Barbie smiled at them. She raised her glass high. "Thanks. And here's to the happiest holiday ever!"